Charlotte in New York

BY JOAN MACPHAIL KNIGHT
ILLUSTRATIONS BY MELISSA SWEET

chronicle books · san francisco

une assiette de crêpes

April 15, 1894
The Buvette de la Plage
Le Pouldu, Brittany

Our hotel is so close to the sea, I can feel salt spray on my face when I open the door. Toby likes it here, I can tell. He barks and runs in circles whenever we step outside.

I like it, too. I have pancakes at every meal—only here they call them "crêpes." Today I had them with strawberry jam for breakfast, with cheese for lunch and with shrimp for dinner. For dessert, I had crêpes with applesauce.

The blacksmith had his hands full this morning! An automobile broke down right in front of his shop. By the time Lizzy and I got there, so had most of the village—even Monsieur Duboc with his herd of sheep, and a girl with ten squawking geese. It's not every day you see an automobile in Giverny—much less a bright yellow one! The blacksmith said the driver was Monsieur Durand-Ruel from Paris. And that if he hadn't been so quick to trade his horse and carriage for a machine, he wouldn't have had to arrive at his hotel "à pied"—on foot—carrying his luggage! Then the blacksmith laughed and hitched his big gray workhorse to the automobile and pulled it to the side of the road.

Papa said Monsieur Durand-Ruel is here to visit his old friend Monsieur Monet. And to look at paintings by the American artists living in Giverny. So many, like Papa, have come to Giverny to learn to paint "en plein air"—outdoors—in the French style called Impressionism. Monsieur Durand-Ruel is planning a show of their work at his gallery in New York and wants Papa's work to be in it. Mr. Foster's, too. I've never been to New York...and I can't wait! I'm so glad the Fosters are coming. Lizzy Foster is my best friend, and it wouldn't be the same without her. Mama says New York is the place to be. Papa says it's nothing like our hometown of Boston—and Lizzy and I will see why when we get there!

I wish we could go right away, but Papa says we're off to Brittany first. Monsieur Durand-Ruel talks about a painter there named Gauguin whose paintings are like no others. Papa wants to see for himself. The Fosters won't be coming. I'll miss Lizzy, but I'll see her on the dock at Le Havre....

And I'm learning to paint like Papa. This morning, we took our easels to the beach. After a while, Marie Henry, the innkeeper, came down. Everyone calls her Marie Poupée because she looks like a little doll. She said something to Papa about "un Parisien"—a man from Paris—and Papa told me he'd be right back. I stayed on the beach to paint.

All at once, a shadow fell on my painting. I looked up and saw a boy standing there. He said his name was Hippolyte. He told me he's French but he can speak English as well as any American. Then he told me he had a bucketful of sardines. I could smell them! When I told him I was going to New York, he laughed, pointed to the bucket, and said, "If wishes were fishes, I'd go to New York, too!" And then he walked away.

un seau plein de sardines

When Papa got back, he said that the Parisien, Monsieur Durand-Ruel, has to leave for Paris tomorrow. If Papa wishes to meet Monsieur Gauguin, he'll have to arrange it on his own. Then Papa looked at his canvas and said, "The light's changed; I'll finish in the morning." We went up to the hotel and had lunch on the terrace.

le poisson de mer

les algues

l'oursin

Every day, Marie Poupée teaches me some French words she thinks I should know.

l'hippocampe

le château de sable

la barque de pêche

April 24, 1894
The Buvette de la Plage
Le Pouldu, Brittany

We still haven't seen Monsieur Gauguin—not once. At dinner tonight, Papa asked Marie Poupée what she knew about him. She said he is "très difficile," very difficult. She must like his paintings, though. The walls are covered with them. The windows, too. He painted right on the glass so you can't see out. "Another brilliant painter who can't pay his hotel bills," said Papa. Then he stood up to stretch. Papa looks like a giant in the little dining room. It's no bigger than my bedroom in Giverny. The tables and chairs are so tiny he has to eat with his knees at his chin. It's not comfortable for him, but for me it's as cozy as can be.

Mama is going to Giverny tomorrow to help Raymonde pack our things. Then on to Paris to buy clothes for New York. She says New Yorkers are crazy for anything with a French label in it, and she'll have the "crème de la crème," the best of the best. I hope she finds a beautiful dress for me. I bet she will!

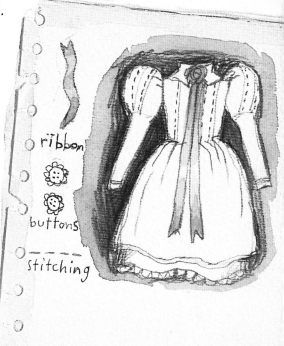

ribbon

buttons

stitching

April 29, 1894
The Grands Sables beach
Le Pouldu, Brittany

Today we finally saw Monsieur Gauguin! He was sitting on a rock at the top of the cliffs along the beach. The wind caught his black cape—he looked like a huge bat hunched over his sketchbook. Maybe even a vampire!

Papa told me Monsieur Gauguin likes to say, "I close my eyes to see." That means he paints from his imagination. He doesn't set up his easel outdoors to paint what's before him the way the Impressionists do. He takes his sketchbook back to the studio and makes his paintings there. Not only that, he won't mix colors and paint things as they really look—he doesn't care about that. He uses pure color, right from the tube.

When Monsieur Gauguin saw us looking at him, he put his sketchbook under his arm and marched away. "Now there's a man who doesn't want to be bothered," said Papa.

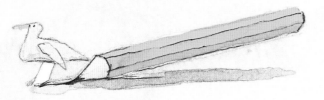

May 2, 1894
The Buvette de la Plage
Le Pouldu, Brittany

Papa excused himself before dessert tonight to work on his painting. I wasn't ready to leave the dining room—not with Monsieur Gauguin at the next table! And Marie Poupée's "Crêpes Sauterelles" still to come for dessert. She calls them "Grasshopper Crêpes" because they jump high in the air when she flips the pan to turn them over. Then she fills them with pears cooked in sugar and butter. Yummy!

I knew Monsieur Gauguin was a woodcarver as well as a painter, but I was surprised to see he had carved geese and cherries on his "sabots," his wooden shoes. And painted the geese white with yellow feet, and the cherries bright red!

Monsieur Gauguin is mean. He doesn't like dogs very much—and dogs don't like him! When he stood up to leave, Toby growled. Monsieur Gauguin raised his cane as if to hit Toby, then marched out of the room. His cane is carved, too—green frogs and a serpent with a twisty red tongue.

I want to tell Papa, but that will have to wait. He's busy making a painting of the cottage we pass on our way down to the beach. He says that, although it may seem easy, it's really very difficult to choose colors that are different from the ones in the landscape and still have them look convincing on the canvas, as if they belong there. I think I'll try that myself.

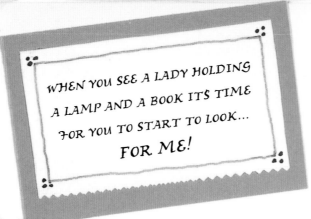

WHEN YOU SEE A LADY HOLDING A LAMP AND A BOOK ITS TIME FOR YOU TO START TO LOOK... FOR ME!

May 4, 1894
The Buvette de la Plage
Le Pouldu, Brittany

On my breakfast tray this morning was an envelope addressed to "Mademoiselle Charlotte." With this mysterious note inside.

I asked Marie Poupée whom it was from. "Aucune idée!"—No idea!—she said, and hurried out. I can't wait to show it to Lizzy. Now I have to hurry. We're off to Le Havre to catch the ship to New York. It takes two whole days to get there, and Papa wants to get an early start.

Le Mont-Saint-Michel

By the side of the road
Somewhere in France

I'm glad we stopped to change horses. I can't write in the coach—Toby likes to sit on my lap and look out the window. We just saw a fairy castle rising out of the sea. Papa says it's really a village called Le Mont-Saint-Michel. When the tide comes in, the village is surrounded by water. When the tide goes back out, there's nothing but quicksand all around. The fishermen must know where it's safe to wade—at least I hope they do!

No wonder Papa chose this hotel. Lots of painters stay here, including our neighbor in Giverny, Monsieur Monet! I saw him playing dominoes under the apple trees. When I told him I'm going to New York, he said he had never been. And would I bring him back "un petit quelque chose"—a little something. I promised I would. Papa says you can find anything under the sun in New York. What will I find, I wonder?

Honfleur harbor at low tide

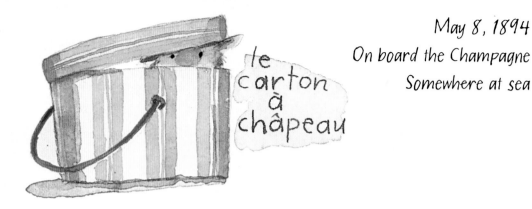

le carton à châpeau

May 8, 1894
On board the Champagne
Somewhere at sea

I was so happy to see everyone at the dock, especially Lizzy. And Mama brought Raymonde! I would have missed her cooking if she had stayed behind in Giverny. When I asked if she would miss France, she said, "pas du tout,"—not at all—she's on her way to "l'Amérique"!

Raymonde and I are sharing a cabin. Every day, she teaches me some French words, and I teach her some English ones. Toby and I have the upper bunk. I didn't want to put him in the ship's kennel, so I hid him in Mama's hatbox when we came on board. When the coast is clear, Lizzy and I walk him on deck. And we feed him scraps from the table. We put them in our napkins when no one's looking!

I've already met my first New Yorkers: Mr. and Mrs. Havemeyer. They're on their way back to New York with paintings they bought in Paris. They must be very rich. Papa says Mr. Havemeyer is called the "Sugar King." That's because he owns a sugar company. But he certainly isn't sweet, in spite of his name. When Lizzy and I were singing on deck this morning, he snapped his newspaper and told us to be quiet.

Mrs. Havemeyer is nice, though. She is a good friend of the famous American artist Miss Mary Cassatt and owns a lot of her paintings. She says Miss Cassatt often paints pictures of mothers and children and showed us a small one of her with her daughter, Electra. She says Miss Cassatt gets so seasick she has to be carried off the ship when it docks. Even when it's a calm crossing! Poor Miss Cassatt!

Lizzy and I have been all over this ship looking for a lady holding a lamp and a book. We've seen many ladies holding books, but all the lamps are nailed (or fastened) down in case of rough weather.

When I got dressed for dinner tonight, Papa said I looked pretty as a picture. Then he painted a quick picture of me. I asked if it would be in the exhibition. He said no, this painting is not for sale. I'm glad—I'm wearing a dress Mama brought me from Paris, the frilly white one with the black velvet sash.

It's our last night at sea, and the captain invited the Fosters and us to dine at his table. He's very handsome in his navy blue uniform with lots of gold braid. When Mama held up a pearl she found in one of her oysters, he said, "Beauty contemplates beauty," and made her blush.

Raymonde and Toby are fast asleep. I hope I can sleep, too. We'll sail past the Statue of Liberty at dawn—I don't want to miss that! Papa says the statue is a present from the people of France to the people of the United States. And the skeleton of steel that holds her up was designed by Monsieur Gustave Eiffel, the man who built the Eiffel Tower.

PAQUEBOT DE LA Cⁱᵉ Gˡᵉ TRANSATLANTIQUE ENTRANT A NEW-YORK

Goodnight, fishes in the sea.
Good morning, Statue of Liberty!

Brooklyn Bridge. N. Y. City.

May 14, 1894
New York harbor

The ship's whistles woke us this morning. Everyone was on deck to be the first to see the Statue of Liberty. It was so foggy, I was afraid we'd sail right past without even seeing her! Then Papa whispered, "Look for the light in her lamp." All at once I saw it. "There she is!" I cried. As we got closer, the fog lifted, and we saw the biggest statue in the world. Fifteen stories high, with an island all to herself to stand on! Monsieur Bartholdi, the sculptor, made her out of copper and gave her his mother's face—a very beautiful one.

As we sailed by, I saw she was holding a lamp in one hand and a book in the other! Then Lizzy shouted, "There's New York!" And I saw the city straight ahead. As we got closer, we saw that New York has the busiest harbor, the biggest ships, the tallest masts and the most flags flying. And the longest bridge in the world, the Brooklyn Bridge. More than a million people live in New York, and now I'll be one of them!

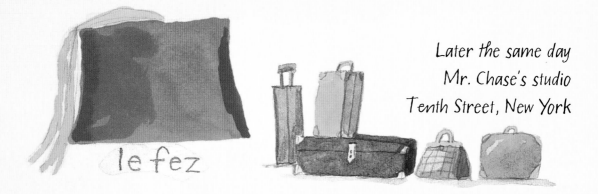

le fez

Later the same day
Mr. Chase's studio
Tenth Street, New York

There were so many people at the dock, it looked as if all of New York had come to meet us. Even so, we had no trouble spotting Papa's old friend Mr. William Merritt Chase. He was wearing a red Arab hat (a "fez," Papa says!) and a long black cape, lined with crimson. Beside him stood two enormous dogs—Russian wolfhounds—as white as snow. Toby wanted to play, but they looked down their long noses at him.

Mr. Chase has found an apartment for us to share with the Fosters. We haven't seen that yet—the carriage brought us here instead. I've never had such an exciting ride! Lizzy and I loved it. Mama is still trying to catch her breath. Everybody is in a hurry—carriages, omnibuses, bicycles and coaches race at full speed, ringing bells. Our carriage, with four shiny black horses, galloped past them all! And trains run high overhead. I never saw that before! They clang and screech and leave a trail of sparks and ashes on the street below. Papa says the train is called "the el" (for "elevated") and that it

Elevated Curve, New York.

runs so close to the buildings, you can look out the train window and see what people are having for dinner.

      Mama tells me that Mr. Chase's studio is the talk of the town, and no wonder! Everywhere are costumes of velvet and silk, sparkling jewels, masks and marionettes, paintings and tapestries—even a big swan with a black beak and a pink flamingo (stuffed!). Not only that, Mr. Chase does more than paint in here— he gives parties and hires a beautiful Spanish dancer to entertain his guests. Her name is Carmencita, but people call her "The Pearl of Seville." Best of all, Mr. Chase told Papa he won't be needing the studio this summer—he'll be teaching at a painting school on Long Island. Papa can have the studio all to himself.

May 19, 1894
24 Fifth Avenue
New York

Lizzy and I can't wait to explore New York. From *the* window, we see that everybody has someplace special to go and something special to do. Everybody except us. Papa and Mr. Foster went to buy painting supplies. Mama and Mrs. Foster are going to the opera tonight and need their beauty rest. And Raymonde is _still_ unpacking the trunks. When we asked her to come for a walk with us, she said, "Il faut patienter." But we can't be patient. We decided to take Toby for a walk and be back before anyone noticed we had gone.

When we got to Mr. Chase's studio, it started to rain. I knocked on the door. There was no answer. As I pushed the door open, a man shouted from inside, "Hold it! Stop right there!" And we did! We didn't move a muscle for a very long time. Then we peeked in. We saw two girls, standing as still as can be. And, on the other side of the room, Mr. Chase working at his easel. He was painting their portrait.

Later, Cosy Chase, who is our age, told us her father often makes her and her sisters stop in the middle of a game to pose. She doesn't mind, though. She even wears a bit of red every day just in case. Mr. Chase likes a touch of red in all his paintings.

Suddenly there was a loud clap of thunder. Quick as a wink, Toby was out the door and up the street. I was afraid we'd never catch him! But a tall woman— I couldn't see her face, it was so dark—picked him up and held him until we caught up. Then she hailed a carriage and told the driver to take us home. I said, "Thank you, Mrs...." "Miss," she said, "Miss Cassatt." We were so surprised!

When we rang our doorbell, Raymonde answered. She took muddy Toby down to the kitchen for a good scrubbing. "Ne vous inquietez-pas!"—Don't worry!— she said, and promised not to tell.

Toby couvert de boue   le savon

The Fosters had to leave yesterday for Boston. Mr. Foster has business there. I miss Lizzy already!

     I hope they're back in time for the Havemeyers' ball. A footman brought our invitation on a silver tray. Mama has talked of nothing else since she heard about it. And she still hasn't decided what costume to wear! I'm going to be Mademoiselle La La, the famous acrobat at the circus in Paris. The dressmaker is making me a sparkly dress and, for Toby the circus dog, polka-dot pantaloons and a pointy hat to match.

Miss LaBelle
Fine French Fashion

WINDSOR
GLAZED CHINTZ
31 inch width
10025 Egg Plant

WOODSIDE
30057
Ivory

des ombrelles

The Casino Restaurant
Central Park
New York

Papa and I are having lunch with his friend from Boston, Mr. Maurice Prendergast. We met here in Central Park. It took a while to find him; there were so many people. He was finishing a watercolor. Quickly, he painted me in it. My pink parasol, too!

AT THE MENAGERIE
CENTRAL PARK, NEW YORK

On our way here, we passed fields of sheep and goats. We saw camels, too. When the grass gets high, they hitch a camel to a mowing machine and put it to work.

At the menagerie we saw a fat hippopotamus and a buffalo bison named Black Diamond. And elephants belonging to Mr. P. T. Barnum. He keeps them there when his circus isn't traveling. The big birdcage was filled with brightly colored parrots from faraway places. They squawked and screeched so loudly, Mr. Prendergast had to shout to give us news of Monsieur Gauguin. He has sailed away to the South Seas to paint and lives on a sunny island called Tahiti. "Au revoir, Monsieur Gauguin!" Goodbye!

June 16, 1894
24 Fifth Avenue
New York

Tonight was the most special night ever! I'm going to write down everything that happened so I can tell Lizzy about it. Papa was Buffalo Bill. Mama, the beautiful French queen Marie Antoinette. She wore a white powdered wig and a dress so enormous that Papa and I had to stuff her into the carriage. Then there was no room for us! We didn't mind—we sat up top with the driver. He said he would show us the tallest buildings we had ever seen—and he did! They're called "skyscrapers," after the tallest mast on a ship, the one that seems to scrape the sky. Everywhere the carriage went, people stared at us. Papa said it's because Toby barks so loudly, and anyway it's not every day you see a dog wearing pantaloons and a pointy hat, even in New York! But I know better—they thought we _were_ Buffalo Bill and Mademoiselle La La!

The walls at the Havemeyers' are covered with paintings, just like a museum. I saw five of Monsieur Monet's haystack paintings all in a row. When I asked Mrs. Havemeyer why she had so many paintings of the same scene, she said she couldn't make up her mind which one to keep. She smiled when I told her how I peeked over Monsieur Monet's shoulder when he painted those haystacks back in Giverny and how sweet the hay smelled in the hot sun.

When we got to the ballroom, I saw Mrs. Havemeyer's daughter, Electra. I recognized her from the painting Mrs. Havemeyer showed us on the ship. She was wearing a sparkly white dress and a diamond tiara. I guessed she was a princess, but she said she was an electric light! Then she said the dance floor had been polished with oatmeal that morning and did I want to see her glide across it? Before I could answer, she slid across the shiny floor and disappeared into the crowd of dancers.

All at once, Toby jumped out of my arms and ran to a tall woman wearing a mask of blue-black feathers. She might have been a raven—I couldn't tell. She bent down to pick Toby up, and he covered her with kisses. It was Miss Cassatt! Mama said she had never known Toby to behave that way with a complete stranger. Then the "complete stranger" handed him back to me with a smile—and a wink, I think. I couldn't be sure with all those feathers.

That's when I saw the Statue of Liberty! And, beside her, a sea captain not much taller than I, with gold braid on his white hat and jacket. When I got closer, I saw the sea captain was Hippolyte! He laughed at my surprise and told me that he's the one who put the note on my breakfast tray in Brittany. In fact, he and his uncle, Monsieur Durand-Ruel, travel to New York so often, they keep a boat here. And would I like to see it?

Just then, out came the Pearl of Seville. She danced and twirled, and when it was over, people threw flowers and money at her feet. Bracelets, too! Papa says the famous portrait painter Mr. John Singer Sargent had a difficult time when he set out to paint her portrait—he couldn't get her to stand still!

Marie Antoinette
wig

Monsieur Durand-Ruel came for me this morning in a shiny red carriage pulled by a high-stepping black horse with red feathers in its mane. He said Hippolyte had gone to the yacht club and that he would take me there. But first he needed to stop at the Metropolitan Museum of Art.

MUSEUM OF ART, CENTRAL PARK, N. Y. CITY.

The Metropolitan Museum of Art

No museum is as large as the Louvre in Paris, but the Metropolitan Museum of Art comes close! While Monsieur Durand-Ruel talked to the curator, I explored. Before I knew it, I was alone in a great hall filled with paintings and sculptures as far as I could see. Just when I thought I would never find my way back to Monsieur Durand-Ruel, he and the curator came around the corner. When I asked if there were any paintings by Monsieur Monet, Monsieur Durand-Ruel said, "Not yet—but there will be soon. We were just talking about that."

When we got to the carriage, Monsieur Durand-Ruel told the driver to take us to Central Park. I was surprised—I thought we were on our way to the river for a sail! The carriage stopped by a little pond with toy sailboats on it. All at once, I saw Hippolyte with a long stick, lining up a sailboat for the start of a race. "So this is the

the sailboat pond

boat they keep in New York," I thought to myself. All at once, the boats' sails filled with wind, someone shouted, "They're off!" and Hippolyte waved to me.

After the race, I told Hippolyte I can sail a real sailboat. Even at night. I know how to find my way by the stars. Papa taught me at Appledore Island. When I asked if I could sail his boat, Hippolyte said girls aren't allowed—the yacht club is for men only. I must have looked disappointed. "Allons-y,"—Let's go—he said, and led me to a big lake with rowboats for rent.

Hippolyte says even the lakes and ponds in Central Park are man-made. There was nothing here but swampy land until Mr. Calvert Vaux and Mr. Frederick Law Olmsted designed meadows, gardens and woodlands with roads, tunnels and bridges. It took 3,600 men to build it all!

Now we're letting the boat drift while Hippolyte looks for fish. All the rowboats are named after flowers. Ours is called Violet. I wish this day would never end....

le canot

le bouquet de violettes

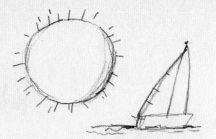

July 20, 1894
24 Fifth Avenue
New York

Raymonde says, "Il fait chaud, chaud, chaud," and it _is_ hot, hot, hot. When I got
to the studio today, Papa was painting in his underwear. He told me he was
painting from memory. "Thinking of cooler climes," he added. When I asked
what that meant, he turned the canvas toward me. It was Marie Poupée and
her dog Limouzin. Papa was remembering the cool sea air in Le Pouldu and how
Limouzin would run to greet everyone who came to stay at the inn under the
pines. All at once, Papa put his paintbrush down. "Enough of this heat," he said.
"Appledore Island, here we come!"

les mouettes

I ran home to tell Mama and Raymonde, and when I got there, I found a postcard waiting for me. From Lizzy. From Appledore!

On the back it says:
Windswept cottage, Appledore Island.
Everybody misses you. Me most of all! When are you coming?
Love, Lizzy

There isn't time to write her back. She'll be so surprised to see me!

When I told Hippolyte we were going to Appledore, he said he and Monsieur Durand-Ruel were off to San Francisco. Then he pulled an egg from his pocket. "It's so hot," he said, "I can fry this on the sidewalk." And he did! We put the egg on a plate to cool, and Toby gobbled it up. I have so much to tell Lizzy....

August 1, 1894
Appledore Island
The Isles of Shoals

I'm so happy to be back in Appledore! To get here, we had to take a train from New York to Boston, then another from Boston to Portsmouth, New Hampshire. When we stepped from the train at Portsmouth harbor, a gust of wind came up and blew our hats into the water. We didn't mind—we could smell salt air and hear gulls screeching overhead. And see the steamboat Pinafore waiting to take us out to Appledore.

une assiette
de praires

la louche

le couteau

When we got to our cottage, Raymonde opened the shutters and windows and let the sunshine in. We haven't been here for two years, but everything looks just the same. Toby and I raced to the Fosters'. He got there first and leapt into Lizzy's arms. She was so glad to see us!

Tonight we went to Appledore House for dinner. Everyone was there, including the poet Mrs. Celia Thaxter with her houseguests. She always has lots of those—artists, other poets and musicians, mostly. Raymonde said the clam chowder was "beau et bon"—beautiful to look at _and_ good to eat. Then she disappeared into the kitchen and came out with the recipe for the chowder and the peach crisp!

After dinner, we sat by the fire and listened to island stories. One was about a ghost who haunts the hotel, an old lady who warms her toes by the fire. Then Mrs. Thaxter told us about a wild storm they had when she was a girl, when her father was the lighthouse keeper here—the wind was so strong, they had to bring the cow into the kitchen so she wouldn't blow out to sea!

un bol de pêches

⟫⟫ Recipe for Peach Crisp ⟪

Preheat oven to 375°

Make a topping with

1/2 cup flour

1/2 cup brown sugar

4 tablespoons salted butter, cut in bits

Using your fingertips, work ingredients together until they form small clumps. Refrigerate while you prepare the peaches: Take 6 or 8 peaches, peeled and sliced, and put them in a buttered pie pan. Sprinkle the topping over the fruit and bake 35-40 minutes, until the topping is golden and the juices bubble. Serve warm with vanilla ice cream.

August 12, 1894
Appledore Island
The Isles of Shoals

I went to meet the mail boat this morning and saw a strange-looking package for Mrs. Thaxter—a box of dirt with wire across the top. I told the mailman I'd take it straight to her.

Mr. Childe Hassam

When I got to Mrs. Thaxter's house, Papa's old friend Mr. Childe Hassam was on the porch. He was signing his name to a painting he had just finished. Next to it, he put a red crescent moon. When I asked if he knew where Mrs. Thaxter was, he said, "Try the parlor."

There were so many flowers in the room that I couldn't see her at first. Then I spotted her. She was lying down, reading a book. When I handed her the box, she exclaimed, "Come with me!" and took me out to her garden.

"Poor, dry, dusty creatures," she said as she put the box down and sprinkled it with water from a watering can. All at once, I heard the high peeping sound of many little voices. She removed the wire and turned the box on its side. Out hopped what must have been a hundred tiny toads. "I ordered them from the mainland," she said, "to feast on my pesky slugs. Before long, the toads will grow as large as apples, and there won't be a single slug left in my garden." Now I know why I saw toads for sale at markets in France!

Mrs. Thaxter loves poppies, too, and has lots of different kinds.

I told her how I sowed poppy seeds Monsieur Monet gave me over the snow in my garden in Giverny. She said that in February, when it's still very cold, she plants poppies, too. But she plants them this way:

Half-fill a shallow box with sand. Set rows of empty eggshells close together in the sand, each shell cut off at one end, with a drainage hole at the bottom. Fill the shells with clean earth and sow a poppy seed in each. Keep damp and place in a sunny window. When seedlings are ready to plant in spring, gently remove the shell from the earth so as not to disturb the roots. Plant in the ground and water.

des crapauds qui sautent

cut here

earth

seed

Today at the ledges, Papa introduced me to Mr. J. Appleton Brown. He comes every summer to give painting lessons to Mrs. Thaxter. Papa says everybody calls him "Appleblossom Brown" because he likes to paint apple orchards. I wonder if I'll have a nickname one day for what I like to paint best.

He was making a watercolor, and Papa and I set up our easels. I squeezed the colors of Appledore onto my palette:

sea green

seagull white

sandpiper gray

morning glory blue

Tonight we're having a clambake on Smuttynose Island. Lizzy and I will find driftwood for the fire. Seaweed, too, for steaming lobsters and clams. I heard everybody is coming—they're bringing out the whaleboats to ferry people across the channel. But we'll sail out in our little boat, the Skimmer. Papa is down in the cove getting her ready. I'd better hurry! He wants to leave on the tide.

les éléphants

September 7, 1894
24 Fifth Avenue
New York

Papa and Mr. Foster are so excited about the paintings they made in Appledore that we all rushed back to New York so they could include them in the exhibition. I don't mind a bit—the circus is in town! This morning, Raymonde took Lizzy and me to Madison Square to see the parade, and what a parade it was! "Four hundred horses, twenty elephants and one thousand performers," a policeman next to us shouted over the brass band, "nothing like it anywhere else in the world." When it was over, the parade marched into Madison Square Garden and disappeared.

Madison Square Garden

Tonight we went to the performance. The policeman was right! I've never seen such a big circus—three rings, two stages and a ceiling full of acrobats, all going on at once! I didn't know which way to look. Raymonde said, "C'est formidable!"—that's terrific!—over and over again. And it was.

I even found something at the circus for Monsieur Monet—a new American candy called Good and Plenty. It's delicious, and he won't find it in Paris!

GOOD AND PLENTY 5¢

bon
et
beaucoup

barbe à papa

anis

October 10, 1894
24 Fifth Avenue
New York

Tonight was the exhibition. It was a big success! Lots of paintings sold, including Papa's paintings from Brittany and Appledore. Monsieur Durand-Ruel looked very pleased, and he invited everybody to dinner at Delmonico's afterward. Mama was excited because President Cleveland was there. Lizzy and I didn't care about him—the famous reporter Miss Nellie Bly was at the next table. She took a trip around the world in just seventy-two days, the fastest time ever—a world record! She traveled by ship, train, horse, rickshaw, tugboat, sampan and donkey. I have the "Around the World with Nellie Bly" board game.

Monsieur Durand-Ruel ordered oysters and champagne for the table. Mr. Hassam made a toast to "Our art and our travels!" And Mr. Louis Sonntag raised his glass to "the great city of New York and all who paint her!" Everybody cheered and clinked glasses. Mr. Prendergast told us that when Mr. Sonntag was only thirteen, he made a painting of the Brooklyn Bridge, and it was exhibited at the National Academy of Design.

I drank my champagne but gave my oysters to Hippolyte. After that, we had "lobster à la Newburg." And, for dessert, "baked Alaska." "La spécialité de la maison!"—the specialty of the house—said Monsieur Durand-Ruel. And no wonder, with yummy ice cream and sponge cake on the inside and flaming meringue on the outside. While Mr. and Mrs. Havemeyer were busy talking, Electra ordered three more for our end of the table!

des huitres   le champagne   le homard

When we got home, Papa and Mama stayed up late talking. I tried to stay awake so I could hear what they were saying. But I couldn't, and when I came to breakfast there was a painting of me sound asleep in the parlor. Papa must have stayed up all night to paint that. No wonder he's still asleep!

le dindon   les patates   la tarte à la citrouille

For days, Raymonde has talked of nothing but "dindon," "patates" and "tarte à la citrouille."

She never cooked a Thanksgiving dinner before, and everything was delicious. Bravo, Raymonde! "Bien fait!" Well done!

Papa's friend from Giverny, Mr. Theodore Butler, came along with the Fosters. He's Monsieur Monet's son-in-law. He's in New York on a painting trip, and Papa invited him to dinner. He brought some paintings to show (I loved the one of the Statue of Liberty!). And news of Monsieur Monet—he's off to paint in Norway in January. The Norwegian queen asked him to come!

When Mr. Butler left, I gave him the Good and Plenty candies to take back to Monsieur Monet. I wrote the label in my best handwriting:

Pour Monsieur Monet
Giverny, France
de la part de Charlotte Glidden

I hope he likes them as much as I think he will!

The next day

When I woke up this morning, Mr. Butler's painting was hanging on my wall! I rushed downstairs to ask Papa about it. He reminded me of the foggy morning we sailed into New York harbor and how I had been the one to see the lady with the lamp and book before anyone else did. "Now she's yours to see any time you want," he said. Thank you, Papa!

nter Scene, Central Park, New York, N. Y.

Central Park in Winter

December 1, 1894
24 Fifth Avenue
New York

Today we had our first snowfall. Mama and I went ice-skating in Central Park. On our way home, we saw Mr. Hassam waving to us from his carriage. He asked Mama if she would mind standing still a moment. "For a quick sketch," he said. Mama didn't mind a bit. Later she told me she was glad she had decided on her favorite Paris coat that day—the pink with white fur.

I peeked inside the carriage and saw that it was filled with painting supplies. Back in Giverny, Monsieur Monet paints in a studio-boat on the river Epte. Here in New York, Mr. Hassam paints in his carriage! When he sees something he wants to paint, he tells the driver to rein in the horses. Then he gets to work. That's how he came to paint a beautiful picture of Mama walking home through the snow.

Papa says he might use the money from the exhibition for a painting trip to England. He hears the light there is like no other. Besides, Mama wants to have her portrait painted by Mr. John Singer Sargent, who lives there. I have to talk to Lizzy about this!

But first I need to buy a new journal. I've already filled this one up, and our adventure has barely begun....

CREDITS

In order of journal entry

April 15, 1894
Berthe Morisot (1841–1895)
Interior of a Cottage, 1886.
Oil on canvas, 20 x 24 inches.
Musée d'Ixelles, Brussels, Fritz
Toussaint Collection.

April 15, 1894
John Singer Sargent (1856–1925)
Young Boy on the Beach, Sketch for
"Oyster Gatherers of Cancale," 1877.
Oil on canvas, 17 ¼ x 10 ¼ inches.
Terra Foundation for American Art, Daniel J.
Terra Collection, 1999.132. Photograph
courtesy of Terra Foundation for American Art.

April 24, 1894
Reconstruction of the dining room at the
Buvette de la Plage. Photograph courtesy of
the Association des Amis de la Maison Marie
Henry, Le Pouldu.

April 29, 1894
Paul Gauguin (1848–1903)
Breton Girls Dancing, Pont-Aven, 1888.
Oil on canvas, 28 ¾ x 36 ½ inches.
Collection of Mr. and Mrs. Paul Mellon.
Image © 2005 Board of Trustees, National
Gallery of Art, Washington, D.C.

May 2, 1894
Paul Sérusier (1863–1927)
Thatched Cottage with Three Ponds, 1889–90.
Oil on canvas, 28 ¾ x 36 ¼ inches.
Private collection.

May 8, 1894
Mary Cassatt (1844–1926)
*Portrait of Louisine Havemeyer and Her
Daughter Electra,* 1895.
Pastel on paper, 24 x 30 ½ inches.
Copyright © Shelburne Museum,
Shelburne, Vermont.

May 13, 1894
William Merritt Chase (1849–1916)
Dorothy, 1902.
Oil on canvas, 72 x 36 inches.
Indianapolis Museum of Art, John Herron
Fund.

May 19, 1894
Childe Hassam (1859–1935)
Sunday on Fifth Avenue, circa 1890–91.
Watercolor on paper, 30 ½ x 19 inches.
Transparency courtesy of James Graham &
Sons, New York.

June 1, 1894
Maurice Prendergast (1858–1924)
The Terrace Bridge, Central Park, 1901.
Watercolor over graphite, on ivory wove paper,
15 ¼ x 22 ½ inches.
The Olivia Shaler Swan Memorial
Collection, 1939.431. Reproduction,
The Art Institute of Chicago.

June 16, 1894
John Singer Sargent (1856–1925)
La Carmencita, 1890.
Oil on canvas, 90 x 54 ¼ inches.
Musée d'Orsay, Paris. Photograph: Gerard
Blot. Copyright © Réunion des Musées
Nationaux / Art Resource, New York.

July 20, 1894
Pierre Bonnard (1867–1947)
Woman with Dog, 1891.
Oil on canvas, 16 x 12 ¾ inches.
Sterling and Francine Clark Art Institute,
Williamstown, Massachusetts, 1979.23.

August 12, 1894
Hassam painting on the porch of Celia
Thaxter's cottage, Appledore, Isles of Shoals,
circa 1890.
Milne Special Collections, University of
New Hampshire Library, Durham,
New Hampshire.

October 10, 1894
James McNeill Whistler (1834–1903)
Note in Red: The Siesta, by 1884.
Oil on panel, 8 ⁵⁄₁₆ x 12 inches.
Terra Foundation for American Art, Daniel J.
Terra Collection, 1999.149. Photograph
courtesy of Terra Foundation for American Art.

Thanksgiving Day, 1894
Theodore Butler (1876–1937)
Statue of Liberty in the Mist, 1899.
Oil on canvas, 40 x 30 inches.
Private collection.

All other photographs and ephemera
collection of the author.

THE ARTISTS

FRÉDÉRIC AUGUSTE BARTHOLDI (1834–1904) Sculptor, painter and photographer Bartholdi was born in Colmar, in the Alsace region of France. While on a trip to Egypt in 1855, he became fascinated with colossal sculpture and returned in 1869 with a proposal to build a lighthouse at the entrance to the just completed Suez Canal, in the form of a gigantic draped figure holding a torch. Although that project never happened, his idea would find expression in New York harbor as the Statue of Liberty.

PIERRE BONNARD (1867–1947) Born in Fontenay-aux-Roses, France, Bonnard, the son of a War Ministry official, enrolled in both law school and the Académie Julian. When a poster he designed won a competition, he rented a studio in Montmartre and turned full-time to painting. He studied Japanese prints, admired Gauguin's paintings and joined Sérusier's group, the Nabis, creating designs for posters, stained glass, fans and furniture. Bonnard traveled throughout Europe on painting trips, often with Edouard Vuillard, and became friends with Monet and Renoir.

JOHN APPLETON BROWN (1844–1902) A native of Newburyport, Massachusetts, Brown studied painting in Paris with the Normandy landscapist Emile Lambinet. From 1875 on, he lived in New England, where his beautiful paintings of pastoral scenes in springtime earned him the nickname "Appleblossom Brown." He was a frequent visitor to Appledore Island and a good friend of Celia Thaxter's, to whom he gave painting lessons.

THEODORE EARL BUTLER (1861–1936) A native of Ohio, Butler studied with William Merritt Chase at the Art Students League in New York before traveling to Paris to enroll at the Académie Julian. In 1888, he went to Giverny to paint and became a permanent resident of the village when he married Monet's daughter, Suzanne Hoschedé. He was one of the earliest American Impressionists to paint scenes of New York City and had a one-artist show at the Durand-Ruel gallery there in 1900, which featured a number of his paintings of busy New York harbor and the East River.

MARY CASSATT (1844–1926) Born in Pittsburgh, Pennsylvania, to wealthy parents, Mary Cassatt studied art at the Pennsylvania Academy of the Fine Arts before traveling to Paris to continue her studies when she was twenty-two. She became a close friend of Degas and was a great help to the Impressionists by promoting their work in the United States and convincing rich American friends like the Havemeyers to buy their paintings.

WILLIAM MERRITT CHASE (1849–1916) The son of a shopkeeper, Chase was born and raised in Indiana. He left when he was twenty years old to study at the National Academy of Design in New York. After further study in Europe, he returned to Manhattan, where he transformed a vast space in the old Tenth Street Studios into an exotic showplace that attracted many pupils and lucrative portrait commissions. Quickly, Chase became recognized as a brilliant art teacher and one of the most successful artists of his day. In 1886, he married Alice Gerson, a family friend, and their beautiful children became favorite models for his paintings.

PAUL GAUGUIN (1848–1903) Born in Paris to a French journalist father and a Peruvian mother, Gauguin had a successful career as a stockbroker when he met Camille Pissarro and the other Impressionists and attended their first exhibition. Overwhelmed at what he saw, he retired from business to become a painter, moving out of Paris to Rouen, then Denmark, Martinique and Panama, before settling for several years in the Brittany towns of Pont-Aven and Le Pouldu. In 1895, he moved permanently to the South Sea islands.

(FREDERICK) CHILDE HASSAM (1859–1935) Born in Dorchester, Massachusetts, Hassam traveled to Europe when he was twenty-two to visit museums and spend three years at the Académie Julian in Paris. On his return, he settled in New York, the city he considered to be the most beautiful in the world, and took his subjects from Manhattan's avenues, parks, bridges and squares, often capturing effects of snow or rain. Summers he worked on Appledore Island in the Isles of Shoals, the home of his friend the poet Celia Thaxter. It was she who suggested he drop the name "Frederick" in favor of the more glamorous-sounding "Childe Hassam."

CLAUDE MONET (1840–1926) Oscar Claude Monet was born in Paris but moved to Le Havre with his family when he was five. Even as a boy, he was gifted and encouraged by his parents and teachers to study art. In 1859, he returned to Paris to attend Académie Suisse. In 1862, he met Pierre-Auguste Renoir and Alfred Sisley, and together they founded an independent group of artists. They organized their first group exhibition in 1874. Monet's painting *Impression: Sunrise* gave rise to the name "Impressionism" and defined the group's style. In 1883, after his first wife, Camille, died, Monet moved with Alice Hoschedé and her six children to Giverny. They settled into the Maison du Pressoir, or "Cider-Press House," where he lived—painting, gardening and landscaping—for the next forty-three years.

BERTHE MORISOT (1841–1895) The daughter of a government official who was an amateur painter and supporter of the arts, and the granddaughter of Fragonard, Berthe Morisot was born in Bourges, France. She studied with Camille Corot and Edouard Manet, with whom she had a lifelong friendship. In 1874, Morisot married Eugène Manet, Edouard's younger brother, and had a daughter, Julie, who was often a subject of her paintings. Morisot was the first woman to join the circle of French Impressionist painters and exhibited in all but one of their shows.

MAURICE BRAZIL PRENDERGAST (1858–1924) Maurice Prendergast was born in St. John's, Newfoundland, where his father had a trading post. At the age of ten, he moved with his family to Boston, Massachusetts. In 1891, he and his brother Charles, a frame maker, had saved enough money to travel to Paris, where he enrolled at the Académies Julian and Colarossi. Upon his return to Boston, he visited Manhattan often, where he was inspired to paint many scenes of New Yorkers enjoying themselves in Central Park.

JOHN SINGER SARGENT (1856–1925) Sargent was a brilliant and successful portrait painter. Born in Florence to American parents, he grew up abroad and learned to draw and paint at an early age. Recognizing his son's talent, his father arranged for him to study portraiture under Carolus-Duran in Paris. Sargent became friends with Monet, and the two artists exhibited together and collected each other's work. Sargent traveled extensively throughout his life, capturing in oil and watercolors the scenic places he visited and the friends and family who traveled with him.

PAUL SÉRUSIER (1863–1927) Born in Paris, Sérusier was the son of a wealthy businessman who hoped he would follow him into the perfume business. Sérusier resisted and attended the Académie Julian instead. In Brittany in 1888, Gauguin urged him to paint freely from his imagination, using pure colors. He painted a small wood panel, *The Talisman,* and took it back with him to the Académie Julian where it sparked a controversy. Together with other young painters who admired Gauguin, such as Bonnard, Edouard Vuillard and Maurice Denis, Sérusier formed the group called the Nabis.

W. LOUIS SONNTAG JR. (1869–1898) The son of a successful landscape painter, W. Louis Sonntag Jr. was raised in New York City and painted scenes of New York urban life. A child prodigy with no formal artistic training, he was only thirteen years old when his watercolor of the Brooklyn Bridge was exhibited at the National Academy of Design.

CELIA LAIGHTON THAXTER (1835–1894) Poet and painter Celia Thaxter was born in Portsmouth, New Hampshire. When she was four, she moved with her family ten miles out to sea, to tiny White Island, where her father would be the lighthouse keeper. Eventually he built a popular resort hotel on nearby Appledore Island, where painters such as Hassam and Brown were regular guests. On summer evenings, they, along with other artists, writers and musicians, would gather at Thaxter's cottage where she, in a beautiful white dress, presided over a salon.

JAMES ABBOTT MCNEILL WHISTLER (1834–1903) Born in Lowell, Massachusetts, Whistler moved with his family when he was nine to St. Petersburg, Russia, where his father was a civil engineer for the construction of a railroad line to Moscow. He studied drawing at the Imperial Academy of Science. After several years at West Point Military Academy where he excelled only in drawing, Whistler decided to become an artist and moved to Europe permanently when he was twenty-one. A friend of Gustave Courbet and Edouard Manet, he soon made a name for himself as a talented painter, witty art critic and flamboyant dandy in the style of another friend, Oscar Wilde.

AUTHOR'S NOTE

Charlotte Glidden is not a real girl, although a girl just like Charlotte could very well have traveled with her mother and artist father to France in the 1890s, when American painters flocked there to learn about the new French way of painting called Impressionism. Her journal is based on historical fact. Artists like Mary Cassatt, Theodore Butler and John Singer Sargent traveled to Paris and the beautiful French countryside to paint where French masters painted—in Monet's village of Giverny in Normandy, for instance, and Gauguin's hamlets of Le Pouldu and Pont-Aven on the rocky coast of Brittany. Then, with what they had learned in France, many returned to America in the late 1890s to paint in New York, a great bustling city with more than a million people, soaring skyscrapers and the longest bridges and busiest harbor in the world. American Impressionists such as Childe Hassam, William Merritt Chase and Maurice Prendergast rented apartments and painting studios, often near Washington Square, painted *en plein air* in Central Park, attended exhibitions at the New York gallery of Monsieur Durand-Ruel and were invited to costume balls in grand mansions owned by art patrons such as the Havemeyers. When summer came, they, like the fictitious Glidden family of this book, escaped the city's heat by traveling to picturesque artists' colonies along the seacoast, such as Easthampton, Long Island and Appledore Island, off the coast of New Hampshire.

The author wishes to thank the Pont-Aven Museum, the Metropolitan Museum of Art, the Frick Museum and the Museum of the City of New York for their assistance and access to their

research libraries, as well as to acknowledge Celia Thaxter's book, *An Island Garden,* as a source of inspiration for this book.